The Greatest Gift

Written by
Roxanne Worsham

Illustrated by
Rob Rice

This book is dedicated to every girl and boy in the world!
You are loved!

Published by Worsham Publishing

For more information, contact us:
P.O. Box 421834
Houston, TX 77242

Or visit our website at www.MyDogCanPreach.com

ISBN: 978-1-7364370-3-2

Printed in the United States of America

Other books by Roxanne Worsham
My Dog Can Preach

978-1-7364370-1-8 Hardback
978-1-7364370-0-1 Paperback
978-1-7364370-2-5 E-book

Rob Rice Illustrations
www.robriceillustrations.com

I got a brand-new puppy
I named my new friend Scout

I take him with me everywhere
I love him, there's no doubt

Scout's black and soft
He is small and furry

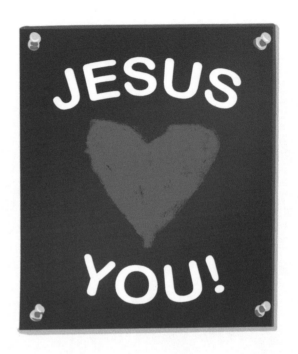

Scout's always playing
And in a hurry

We like to go on adventures
When we take a walk outside

Sometimes we play a game of fetch
Or in my wagon he will ride

He woke me up with kisses
I didn't know what to say!

What a wonderful surprise
To receive this precious pet

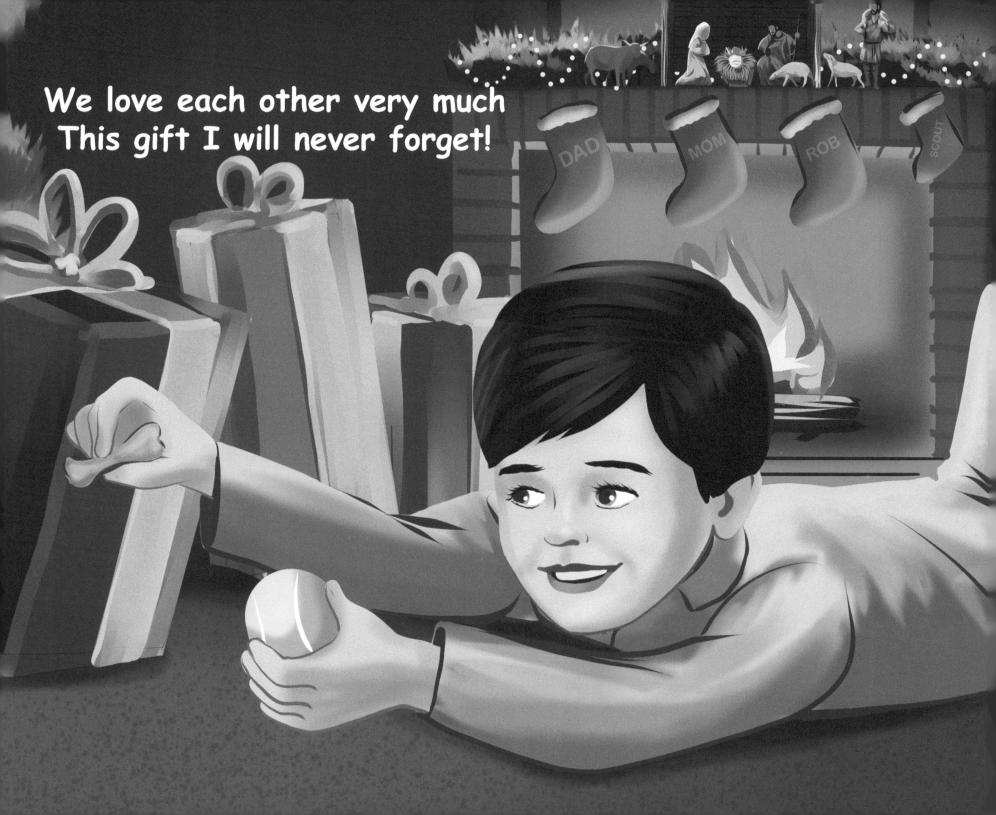

We love each other very much
This gift I will never forget!

My mom told me a story
About another Christmas Day

Of a baby born in a manger
Whose pillow was made of hay

They called His name Emmanuel
Lord of Lords and Prince of Peace

The Alpha and the Omega
His love will never cease

Who loves us more than we can know
Every single boy and girl

How strange to know that the King of kings
Had no place to lay His head

There was a star over Bethlehem
A bright and radiant star

That led the way for travelers
And Wise Men from afar

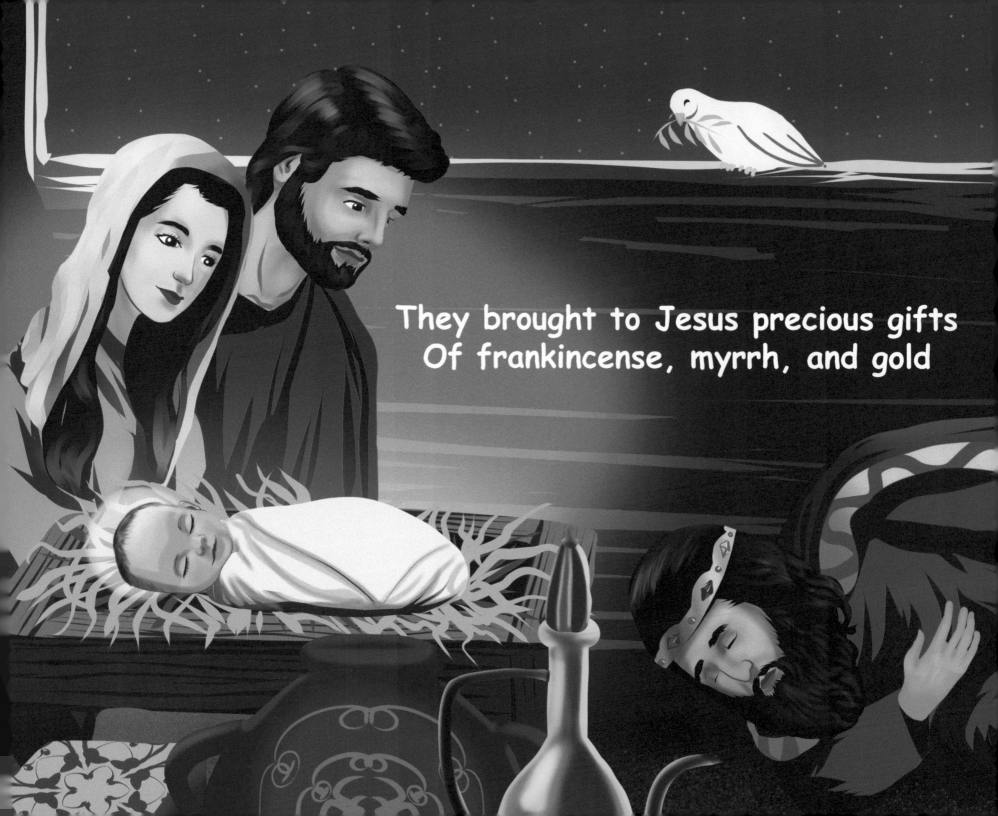

They brought to Jesus precious gifts
Of frankincense, myrrh, and gold

And offer us salvation
Not misery or strife

Be sure and open this present
Because Jesus really loves you

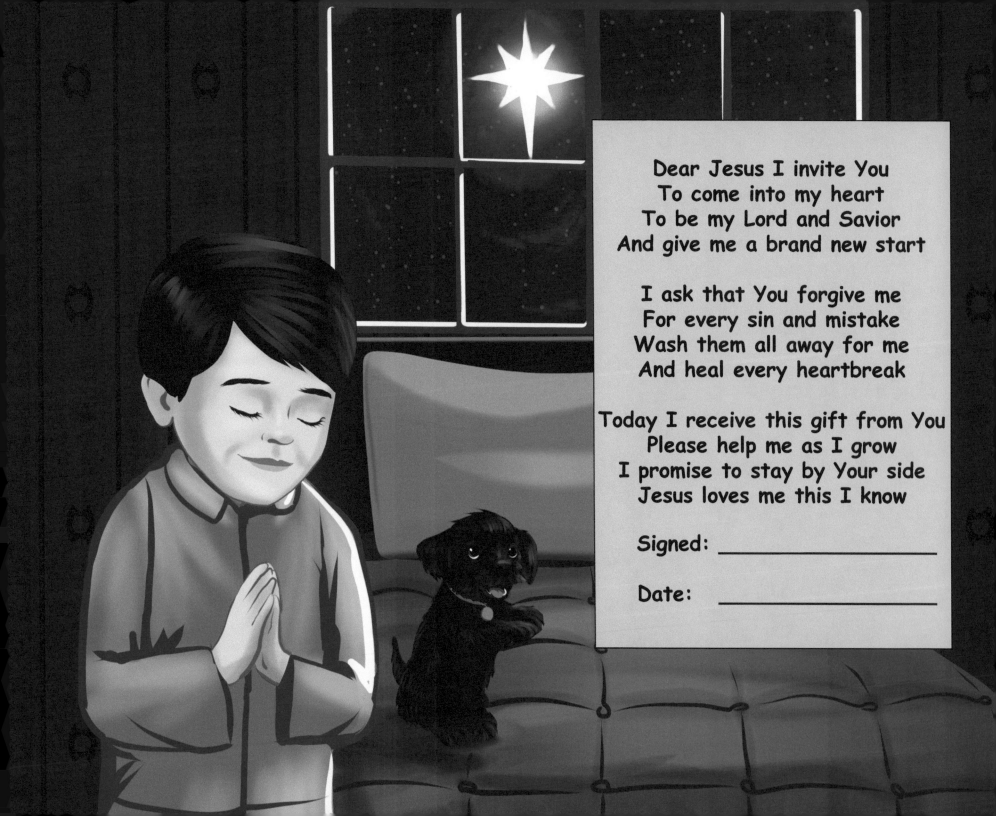

Dear Jesus I invite You
To come into my heart
To be my Lord and Savior
And give me a brand new start

I ask that You forgive me
For every sin and mistake
Wash them all away for me
And heal every heartbreak

Today I receive this gift from You
Please help me as I grow
I promise to stay by Your side
Jesus loves me this I know

Signed: _____

Date: _____

CPSIA information can be obtained
at www.ICGtesting.com
Printed in the USA
BVHW050310151021
618890BV00005B/342